D0095162

One day Dickon leaves his father's geese feeding at the edge of Sherwood Forest, to go in search of Robin Hood.

From his look-out, high in a tree, Dickon overhears the outlaws talking. And then his adventure really begins...

British Library Cataloguing in Publication Data
Collins, Joan,   1917-
    Robin Hood. — (Fables and legends; 7)
    1. Robin Hood — Juvenile literature
    I. Title   II. Hook, Richard   III. Series
    398.2'2   PZ8.1
    ISBN 0-7214-0885-0

First edition

© LADYBIRD BOOKS LTD MCMLXXXV

ROBIN HOOD

written by Joan Collins
illustrated by Richard Hook

Ladybird Books Loughborough

In the Greenwood

It was very early in the morning. Dickon had come to Sherwood Forest to find Robin Hood. He was eight years old, with a snub nose, freckles and ginger hair. There was a hole in one knee of his long stockings, and he had torn his tunic, climbing trees.

Robin Hood was his hero. He knew lots of songs about the tricks Robin had played on the

Sheriff of Nottingham. Dickon's father had told
him that Robin was the best archer in all
England. Dickon wanted to join the band of
outlaws, and shoot with a bow and arrow, too.

So he left his father's geese, feeding at the edge
of the forest, and started to go deeper into
Sherwood. It was dangerous. If the Sheriff's
men caught him, he would be whipped!

Now he was perched high up in a stout oak-tree, hiding in the leafy branches. He looked down into a clearing. A spotted deer and her fawn were feeding quietly in the green shade.

Sherwood belonged to the king, Richard the Lion Heart. He was away, fighting in the Crusades. His brother, Prince John, and the powerful Norman barons had taken over. They would not let the ordinary people go into any of the forests, not even for firewood. They kept them for themselves, to hunt the deer.

Dickon had heard of a hungry peasant whose hand had been cut off for killing a deer for food. Dickon's father said the man was lucky not to have been hanged.

There were men in Sherwood Forest, hiding from Prince John's cruel laws. They were true to King Richard. Robin Hood, their leader, had been wrongly accused of killing the king's deer.

His lands had been taken away. If he had not escaped into the forest in time, he would have been hanged.

'Robin's our friend!' said Dickon's father. 'He takes money away from the rich and gives it to the poor. But he never harms an honest man!'

All these tales made Dickon even more determined to meet the outlaws. But there was no sign of them as he peered down from the tree. The forest was still.

Robin Hood and his outlaws

Suddenly, there was a crash in the undergrowth. The startled deer pricked up their ears and darted off. Dickon was so surprised that he nearly fell out of his tree!

A strong, tall man dressed in green, with a feather in his cap, and a sheaf of arrows at his back, leaped lightly out into the clearing.

'This way!' he shouted over his shoulder.

A slim boy, holding a bow and arrow, followed eagerly on his heels.

'Too late!' the lad cried, shrilly.

Dickon realised, from the voice, that it was a girl dressed as a boy! This must be Robin Hood and Maid Marian! Robin had rescued Marian, when her father wanted her to marry a rich old man. Then Robin had brought her to the Greenwood.

A fat jolly friar in a full brown robe waddled into sight. He was followed by a rough great fellow, nearly seven feet tall, who carried a thick quarterstaff.

The four sat down on the grass to rest.

'Give us one of your venison pasties, Marian!' said the friar, taking a drink from a flask at his belt.

'You're always hungry, Friar Tuck!' laughed the girl. 'You'll have to do better at hunting! Our larder's nearly empty!'

'Is there any news from Nottingham today, Little John?' asked Robin.

'Something that will please you, Robin!' said the giant. 'The Sheriff is offering a prize for the best archer at the Goose Fair – tomorrow. It's a silver arrow! All the bowmen in the shire are going to shoot for it.'

'And I shall be there!' said Robin, gaily.

'No! You mustn't go!' cried Marian. 'If you're caught, you'll be hanged!'

'That won't stop me!' said bold Robin Hood. 'I've fooled the Sheriff before, and I can do it again! Remember when I dressed up as the hangman, Little John?'

'Yes! You tied the Sheriff up, and set all his prisoners free!' chuckled Little John.

'Never fear, Marian!' said Robin. 'I'll bring you home the Silver Arrow tomorrow night! And then we'll have a feast to celebrate.'

And they went off through the trees, talking softly about their plans for the next day.

When they'd gone, and
the forest was quiet
again, Dickon slid down
from his tree. His father
was taking his master's
geese to market at the
fair tomorrow. If Dickon
could go too, he
would be able to watch
the competition for the
Silver Arrow.

'I know Robin Hood
will win!' he said to himself
excitedly as he hurried home.

At the Goose Fair

Dickon had never been to a fair before! The market place was crowded, noisy and exciting. He stopped at a pastry cook's stall and bought a delicious piece of spicy gingerbread sticky with honey.

He munched away, watching a juggler catch knives in his mouth. There were tumblers too, in red and yellow, turning head-over-heels on a mat. And girls and boys were dancing to the music of a pipe and a drum. Beggars crouched on the cobblestones, holding out cups for money.

In one corner of the market place they were roasting a whole ox on a spit, over a charcoal fire. It smelled so good that Dickon's mouth watered.

A ballad singer nearby picked out a tune on his harp. *'I'll tell you a tale of bold Robin Hood!'* he sang.

Robin Hood! Dickon jumped. He had forgotten what he had come for!

'Hurry up! You'll be late for the Silver Arrow competition!' said a boy, pointing to the castle courtyard. 'It's over there!'

Dickon ran off after him.

At Nottingham Castle

The Silver Arrow competition was the most
exciting event of the fair. There was standing
room only in the courtyard. Some men were
even perched high up on top of the grey stone
walls. Just after Dickon arrived, the heavy
wooden gates were barred.

The Sheriff of Nottingham, in his long red robe and gold chain of office, was on a high seat in the centre of the platform, surrounded by his important friends.

On a purple velvet cushion, in front of him, lay the Silver Arrow, glittering with jewels.

Dickon managed to wriggle into the front row. He squeezed in next to a fat market woman with a basket of eggs on her arm. The first part of the contest was over. There were only three competitors left.

Men were busy taking down the big round targets with their coloured rings. Instead, they put up three thin white sticks. These were peeled willow wands and very difficult to hit.

Dickon looked round eagerly for Robin Hood and his men. He could see none of them. There were grim men-at-arms by the gates and among the crowd. They looked as if they expected trouble.

The Sheriff was looking round, too, and whispering to the nobleman next to him.

'Who's that man?' Dickon asked the egg woman.

'That's Sir Guy of Gisborne. He's the one who had our Robin Hood made an outlaw! He's a great friend of the Sheriff's!' she said.

Dickon wondered why Robin was not here. He could not understand it.

The Silver Arrow

The three archers were standing ready. One was a Frenchman, a black-bearded man-at-arms, with a short crossbow. He served Guy of Gisborne. The nobles were betting on him.

The second was Simon, a local man, with an English longbow. He was short and bandy-legged, but a good archer. The crowd was on his side.

The third was a stranger, an old man, with a grey beard, a ragged cloak, and a wide brimmed hat. He had surprised everybody with his shooting at the targets. He had hit the gold bull's eye every time.

The Sheriff looked round the crowd. He muttered to Guy of Gisborne.

'Our trap has failed! Robin Hood is not here!'

'He's too much of a coward to show his face!' sneered Guy of Gisborne.

The contest

Then the horn sounded. A buzz ran through the crowd. Dickon stood on tiptoe to watch.

The Frenchman was the first to shoot. His arrow fell just wide of the mark. Guy of Gisborne frowned, but the crowd cheered.

Next came the short Englishman, Simon. He drew his bow and squinted at the mark. The arrow flew straight, grazed the willow wand, but fell to the ground. The crowd groaned.

Then the old fellow stepped forward. He chose his arrow carefully and fitted it to the bowstring. Then he stretched his bow.

It took great strength to draw back a longbow. It was made of stout red yew wood, and was as tall as its owner. You had to use your whole body, not just your arms, to fire it. Would the old man be strong enough?

Dickon noticed his powerful shoulders and keen eye.

ZING! The arrow sped to its mark. It struck the white wand, which split in two! It was a marvellous shot! The old man had won! The crowd went wild.

27

But Dickon was close enough to hear Guy of Gisborne hiss to the Sheriff.

'Only Robin Hood can shoot like that! Look at his hands and wrists! He's not an old man!'

Dickon jumped forward.

'Fly, Robin Hood!' he screamed at the top of his voice. 'It's a trap!'

Guy of Gisborne started to his feet.

'Seize that boy!' he snarled. But Dickon had ducked into the crowd, and scrambled between their legs towards the back of the courtyard.

The escape

On the top of the wall by the gate, twenty bowmen leapt to their feet and trained their arrows on the Sheriff and his friends. They were Robin Hood's men in disguise!

Robin Hood tore off his ragged cloak and false beard and bounded towards the platform. A cheer went up as the people recognised him, in his suit of Lincoln green.

With a mocking bow to the Sheriff, Robin seized the Silver Arrow, and ran back through the crowd.

'After him!' cried the angry Sheriff. 'A hundred pieces of gold for the man who catches him!'

The Sheriff started down the steps from his high seat, but tripped over his long robe. He tumbled head-over-heels to the ground!

Fighting broke out in the crowd; some were trying to help Robin, others wanted the reward.

The men-at-arms stood between Robin and the gate. And then, from nowhere, the giant figure of Little John with his quarterstaff appeared.

One by one, he cracked each man-at-arms on the head, cutting his legs from under him. The Sheriff's men sprawled on the courtyard floor.

The burly figure of Friar Tuck battled through the crowd. Will Scarlet, Much the miller's son, and others followed, fighting off the men-at-arms to join Robin. He had reached the gate but it was barred. There was no time to lose.

A rope swung down from the men at the top of the wall. Robin swarmed up it. Little John, who was wounded, was pulled up to safety by many friendly hands.

Dickon too, had helped. He'd caught the rope and called out to Robin. Just as a man-at-arms grabbed at Dickon, an outlaw snatched the boy up. He tossed him to the top of the wall.

On the other side of the wall, horses were
waiting, with Maid Marian. The outlaws
thundered off for the safety of Sherwood. The
angry cries of the Sheriff's men, who chased
them, died away in the distance.

'What shall I do with the boy?' gasped Will
Scarlet, Robin's second-in-command. He had
scooped Dickon up on to his saddle as he rode
off.

'That boy saved my life!' cried Robin. 'Let his father know he has gone with us, to join in our feast tonight!'

The feast in the forest

The outlaws slowed down to a gentle pace, as they entered the peace of the Greenwood. They took deep breaths of the free forest air.

But Robin knew that they had made Sherwood too hot to hold them. Tomorrow, in the daylight, the Sheriff's men would search every inch of the forest.

'We'll take shelter in the castle of our good
friend, Sir Richard of the Lea,' Robin said, 'and
have Little John and our other wounded looked
after. Then we'll go to our winter quarters in
Barnsdale Forest. But tonight we'll celebrate!'

The outlaws took Dickon to their secret hide-out
among the giant trees. Maid Marian showed him
the one they called 'The Larder Oak'. It was
hollow, and hunks of deer's meat hung from

hooks inside it. 'We'll eat some tonight!' she promised.

One outlaw was sitting making arrows. 'That's Rob the Fletcher,' she said. 'He's fitting goose feathers to the shafts to make sure the arrows fly straight.'

Dickon watched Rob, wishing he could have a bow and arrows of his own.

A charcoal fire was lighted, and great joints of meat put on spits to roast. There was pigeon pie and black bread. The outlaws rolled out a barrel of good English ale and, before long, the feast was in full swing.

Dickon was given the seat of honour, between Robin Hood and Maid Marian. They all drank a health to him.

'Hurrah for Dickon!' cried the outlaws.

The Silver Arrow sparkled as it lay on an old tree stump, in the middle of the feast.

The happy faces of the outlaws shone in the firelight. They called on Alan-a-Dale for a song. He took his harp and sang a new tale – 'Robin Hood and the Silver Arrow.'

'Is it true you first met Little John on a bridge?'
Dickon asked Robin.

'Yes, we had a friendly fight with quarterstaffs,'
said Robin. 'This great lout would not let me
pass!'

'No, I tipped you into the river!' Little John
roared with laughter, cheerful in spite of his
wound.

'Why do you call him *Little* John?' asked
Dickon. 'He's not small at all!'

'That's why!' grinned Robin.

'You look tired, Dickon,' said Maid Marian. The fire had died down and it was getting dark. Dickon was tucked up on a bed of bracken, with a sheepskin over him. The outlaws took turns to keep watch.

At dawn, before the Sheriff's men were about, the outlaws were ready to set forth.

Robin asked Much, the miller's son, to take Dickon home on his way to market. Dickon could hardly believe it was true when Robin gave him a small bow and some arrows to practise with.

'When you're good enough, you can join our band!' Robin promised. 'Remember, you will always have friends in the Greenwood!'

Dickon watched them ride off. He had had such
an exciting adventure. Perhaps one day he
would return to the Greenwood to meet
Robin Hood and his friends again.

Perhaps King Richard would be back on his
throne then, and Robin would not be an outlaw
any more!

Then Dickon wondered if his mother would be
cross about the hole in his stocking!

Stories . . .
that have stood the test of time

Ladybird titles cover a wide range of subjects and reading ages.
Write for a free illustrated list from the publishers:
LADYBIRD BOOKS LTD Loughborough Leicestershire England
and USA – LADYBIRD BOOKS INC Lewiston Maine 04240